William E. Auckland

Letters from the Right Honourable W. E.

on the late political arrangement

William E. Auckland

Letters from the Right Honourable W. E.
on the late political arrangement

ISBN/EAN: 9783337195670

Printed in Europe, USA, Canada, Australia, Japan

Cover: Foto ©Andreas Hilbeck / pixelio.de

More available books at **www.hansebooks.com**

LETTERS

FROM

THE RIGHT HONOURABLE
W——— E——,

ON THE LATE

POLITICAL ARRANGEMENT,

TO THE

EARL OF CARLISLE,	DUKE OF PORTLAND,
LORD NORTH,	LORD LOUGHBOROUGH,
HON. C. J. FOX,	R. B. SHERIDAN, ESQ.
JOHN LEE, ESQ.	J. WEDGWOOD, ESQ.
MR. W. WOODFALL,	WILLIAM ADAM, ESQ.

LONDON:

Printed for S. BLADON, Pater-noster-Row, 1786.

ORIGINAL LETTERS.

LETTER I.

To the EARL *of* CARLISLE,
&c. &c. &c.

Beckenham, Dec. 6, 1785.

My Dear Lord,

EVER anxious to evince my unabating
esteem and inviolable respect for your Lordship, I hasten to impart, by the very earliest
disclosure, an arrangement deeply interesting to both the fortune and the reputation
of him, whom you honour with the sacred
title of Friend.

This moment, my dear Lord, have I ac-
quiesced in Mr. Pitt's respectable and spon-
taneous offer of appointing me Envoy Ex-

B   traordinary

traordinary to the Court of Verfailles, for the purpofe of negociating a eommercial league between the two countries, agreeable to the relevant article of the treaty of Paris. A fituation, my dear Lord, at once amicable and eminent; of Cabinet truft, and diplomatic rank! Poffibly too, of all others, beft adapted to the habits and acquirements of him, who is felected to fulfil it; fince if there be any one point in which both my friends and my enemies unite, I believe it is *my* perfect acquaintance with every art and trick of contraband trade.

As fuch have I acceded to this lofty fituation,—and yet, my dear Lord, with candour will I own, not a few were the diffuafives which I felt ftrong in operation againft fuch numerous and extraordinary allurements.—Might I exprefs it fo, the *bounty* on *my exportation* was, in truth, uncommonly high; but the *countervailing duties* have undoubtedly created a powerful *drawback*. Let thefe, however, be fairly ftated.

It was not the inconfiderate remuneration, which Lord North had fcantily dealt out to me,

me, with his tardy fenfibility, that held me
in a moment's fufpence; as little was it pro-
bable that the falfe fire of many others' re-
proaches, could occafion me one irkfome hour.
To their *mouldable* principles I had but to
ftate my falary; and if their envy could be
lulled, what other paffion had I to fear from
them? No, my dear Lord, it was to you,
and you alone that all my folicitude was
directed—your partiality had twice advanced
me to moft refpectable fituations—we had in
a manner publicly embarked in one common
bottom——you had prefented me to your
friends, and our junction was eftablifhed on
principles declared and unequivocal; tnat
notwithftanding this, I have at once acceded
to a feparate arrangement, is a circumftance
no otherways to be explained, than by de-
claring, as with truth I do, that neither intereft nor vanity have had the fmalleft fhare
in detaching me from your Lordfhip.—No,
upon my honour, I declare, my real motive
was *to fave the State.* In other words, the
fame honeft ardour which incited me to de-
tect and expofe the errors of Adminiftration,
as an opponent, in the courfe of laft feffion,

determined

determined me to prevent them in the en-
fuing, as their friend and affociate. The
latter appeared to me to be a more effectual
way for the country, and in truth, a far better way for myfelf alfo; for to fpeak out, my
dear Lord, my weak enfeebled frame was
but ill-fuited to the vigilance, the eternal
attack, and the impetuous violence of an
oppofition; not to mention the late hours
which a minority debater can lefs reafonably
efcape, but which are the worft on God's
earth for an impaired frame, fuch as I can-
didly admit my own to be. In a word, my
dear Lord, at the clofe of the laft feffions,
what from exceffive fatigue, and the gloomy
profpect of public affairs, I fell into a de-
fpondency too melancholy to paint, but fo
vifible in my countenance, as to alarm my
neareft and deareft connections. My phyfi-
cians advifed the Spa; but my own feelings
convinced me they entirely miftook my cafe.
All this time you were abfent from town,
our commerce expofed to daily and hourly
danger, my reft broken—the country at
ftake—my innocents prattling at my knee,
your favourite Auguftus, the penfive Wil-
helmina,

helmina, and our little playful Federick.
"*I am not made of stone.*"—Jenkinson arrived,
and your friend was vanquished.

No man on earth more cordially detests
deliberate inconsistency than do I, even to
fervour; but, my Lord, my code of private thought is still immutable; nor indeed do I admit a public incongruity, or
even the smallest absence of action con-
sentaneous to profession. What I have
now done, is what I always *had* done before, nay more, what I always will do in
future—to benefit the State, I have accepted
a distinguished office.—Uniform in my earliest idea, "*Non de Republica resperandum*,"
I defy my enemies to pretend that I ever
have hung aloof from even plurality of
office; on the contrary, I do maintain, that
under every conflict, under every change, I
have at all times and with all men inflexibly
retained that eighteen hundred a year, which
I chearfully accepted as an unequivocal
voucher, that no personal bias—no difference
of principle should on any ground detach me
from the public service.

That

That I projected and accomplished *that* coalition, which I now relinquish, I am frank to admit; that as long as I remained with it, I distinguished myself as at least an unwearied searcher of Parliamentary precedents, and a drawer of popular resolutions, I appeal to the fair *unrevised* reports of my speeches, as Mr. Woodfall, *unaided by me*, has transmitted them to posterity; but in answer to all such vexatious observations, permit me to remind your Lordship, that since I presented you with my *five printed letters* (of which a word by the bye) three babes, as your Lordship very well knows, have been added to my former establishment. A *Jus trium*, my Lord, which even in the penal system of party, may not unreasonably mitigate the severer penalties of political commutation! Possibly it may appear but a frivolous detail; yet, alas! my Lord, is it not a melancholy truth, that every article of a nursery apparatus groans under the pressure of accumulated taxation? With the severest œconomy, with even a sumptuary prohibition of the little luxuries, and amusements of puerility,

was

was it poffible for an income of eighteen hundred a year to provide even the neceffary articles of infantine expenditure?

As to my printed letters to your Lordfhip, which poffibly contain fome few ideas not abfolutely illuftrated by my late ftep, is the bafe precedent of Algernon Sidney to be again reforted to? Am I to be criminated by the produ&ion of my own papers? But, in the name of common fenfe, what is the date of thofe letters? Why fo long back as O&ober, 1779; a pretty confiderable diftance to form a criterion of the confiftence or incongruity of a paft with a prefent opinion. Your Lordfhip's well ftored mind will recal the wonderous ftru&ure of the human body, and ably apply it to the exifting cafe. We have it from Pott, that every fingle particle, every individual atom of the body undergoes a complete change within the courfe of five years; and yet the Whimficals of the prefent hour would demand a perfe& famenefs, an entire identity in the light and vòlatile compofition of the mental frame, for not only the fame period, but alfo for an additional
fra&ion

fraction of time, nearly amounting (as some
would calculate it) to another quarterage.
Away with this ineptitude of enmity! The
admirable Horace somewhere obferves,—
" *Ridiculum acri fortius ac melius.*" Yes,
my Lord, your Lordfhip and myfelf will
fcoff at fo unphilofophical an attack, " *Vir-
tute meâ me involvo.*" But I muft now,
reluctantly conclude this imperfect letter. It is my purpofe to enter into an
extended feries of epiftolary ecclairciffement
with many others on the fubject of my apparent aberration from that line of politics
which admitted me to their confidence.—
With your Lordfhip, however, I felt myfelf
irrefiftibly impelled to aufpicate the painful
explanation, " *neque hæc pervulgata effe aut
Tullius reformidet, aut Atticus nolit.*"

I remain, my dear Lord,

Unalterably and faithfully your's,

W———— E——

LETTER II.

To the Right Hon. LORD NORTH,
&c. &c.

Beckenham, December 7, 1785.

My Dear Lord,

THE reiterated proofs of friendship with which you have honoured me, encourage me to hope, that you will hear with pleasure an event in which my interest is materially concerned.

I had yesterday a visit from our old friend Mr. Jenkinson, who came to me with a very obliging and handsome message from Mr. Pitt, offering in the most liberal manner to forget all the little differences of opinion, which arose between us in the course of last session, and to appoint me Envoy Plenipotentiary to the Court of Versailles, to adjust

C and

and conclude a commercial treaty between the kingdoms of France and Great-Britain, according to an article of the late peace, in the parliamentary cenfure of which, I had the fatisfaction of concurring with your Lordfhip. I confefs, that upon the firft mention of this offer, fome doubts fuggefted themfelves to my mind, whether the acceptance of it might not be fubject to an unfavourable conftruction, on the ground of fo flender an appointment occafioning a change of political conduct. But this very natural objection was immediately obviated by Mr. Jenkinfon's informing me, it was Mr. Pitt's intention, that although invefted with the character of Envoy Extraordinary and Plenipotentiary I fhould receive the full appointments of Ambaffador, that is to fay, fix thoufand a year, befides plate, equipage, money, &c. Thefe extraordinary and advanced emoluments have an additional merit which cannot efcape your Lordfhip's obfervation, and which, I truft, your candour will readily believe, was a ftronger incentive to my acceptance of them, than any perfonal or private advantage of my own; I mean the difgrace

which

which they inevitably reflect upon the Minifter; who, while he is perpetually making
profeffions of ftrict œconomy, and patheti-
cally lamenting the impoffibility of confining
the expenditure of the civil lift within due
bounds, lavifhes, without any reafon, fo confiderable a portion of the public money.—
May it not, therefore, be problematical,
whether, by the acceptance of this appointment, I have not more effentially ferved the
caufe I apparently abandon, than I could
have done by the moft ftrenuous and indefa-
tigable perfeverance in oppofition? But, in-
dependently of this confideration, I am per-
fectly fure, my dear Lord, when you confider the fcantinefs of my income (which it
is unneceffary to point out to you, fince,
fuch as it is, I am indebted to your kindnefs
and friendfhip for every fhilling of it)
amounting altogether, including Mrs. Eden's
penfion and my own, together with two fmall
finecure offices, to the annual receipt of
fomething lefs than one thoufand eight hundred pounds, that you will agree with me in
thinking, it would have been abfolute mad-

nefs

nefs on my part, not to have clofed with a propofal fo advantageous.

I cannot, my dear Lord, omit this opportunity of returning you, from the bottom of my heart, the moft fincere and unfeigned thanks, for the many, many favours you have fo kindly heaped upon me, too numerous to be here repeated, too dear to me ever to be obliterated from my memory. If, in return, I have ever had it in my power to render your Lordfhip any fervice, I flatter myfelf you think I have not been neglectful. Upon a late occafion, in endeavouring to remove the difficulties which lay in the way of a reconciliation between your Lordfhip and Mr. Fox, I may, without vanity, boaft of having laboured with zeal and affiduity. It will ever be the pride of my life to have contributed to the union of fuch eminent abilities in the public fervice. You muft recollect, however, my dear Lord, that the avowed object of that meafure was to produce an efficient, vigorous, and, what was more efpecially the anxious wifh of my heart, a *durable* government for this country. That

That object having unhappily proved un-
attainable by the means then propofed, it
would fcarcely be confiftent with my *principles*, to withhold my poor fervices from an
adminiftration, which, though deficient in
point of vigour and ability, with refpect,
however, to that moft effential requifite,
duration, feems at prefent to hold out the
moft flattering profpect. Should I be de-
ceived in this opinion, my dearcft Lord,
need I add, with what cordial alacrity, with
what difinterefted fatisfaction, upon the fup-
pofition of your returning into power, I
fhall haften to tender you once more the
fervices of,

My Dear Lord,

Your moft devoted, moft faithful,

moft obliged, and moft unalterable

humble fervant,

 W——— E——— .

P. S. Mrs. E— defires me to add, that
fhe fhall be proud and happy to execute any
commands at Paris, which Lady North, or
her amiable friends, the young ladies, will
do her the honour to entruft her with.

LETTER III.

TO THE RIGHT HONOURABLE
CHARLES JAMES FOX.

Beckenham, Dec. 7, 1785.

DEAR CHARLES,

MY early habits of intimacy with you, when we were at fchool, and my late habits in politics, fince we have been in oppofition together, call upon me to deal as openly and frankly with you, as it is your general cuftom to do with all mankind. I proceed, therefore, without ceremony, to inform you, that my old friend and neighbour, Mr. Jenkinfon, has moft happily, and entirely reconciled me to my new friend and neighbour, Mr. Pitt. You, who now pafs much of your time in the country, muft be fenfible how irkfome it is not to live upon the moft friendly footing with one's neighbours; and indeed you have one, no farther diftant from

St.

St. Anne's than Windfor, with whom, if you
take my advice, you will, as foon as you
conveniently can, make up all differences;
but of this hereafter. I am convinced the
project is by no means impracticable, unlefs
you prefer a rigid and romantic adherence to
our good friend at Bufhy, which, it is true,
may prove an unfumountable obftacle to it.
Upon the flighteft hint from you, however,
believe me, it is a bufinefs which I fhall
feel myfelf happy to be employed in, and fhall
enter upon that negociation with as much fatisfaction and readinefs as the commercial
treaty, which I am now appointed to adjuft
with the Court of France, although the latter
employment fecures me an income of fix
thoufand pounds a year, with the additional
douceurs of plate, equipage, &c. Such, my
dear Sir, are the firft fruits of the connection
I have now formed ; to fpeak the plain truth,
my political fituation was become fo irkfome
to me, as to affect both my health and fpi-
rits, and even my favourite and beloved re-
treat of Beckenham was become odious to
me, more efpecially as its vicinity both to
Mr. Pitt and Mr. Jenkinfon, perpetually
recalled to my imagination the ftriking,

and

and melancholy difference of our political pofitions.

Quid facerem? neque fervitio me exire licebat,
Nec tam prefentes alibi cognofcere Divos,
Hic illum vidi *Juvenem*, Meliboeæ, quot annis,
Bis fenos cui noftra dies altaria fumant.
Hic mihi refponfum, primus dedit ille petenti:
Pafcite, ut ante, bowes, pueri, fubmittite tauros.

I flatter myfelf, that, although you per-haps may not wholy approve of the ftep I have taken, you will be candid enough to acknow-ledge, that I was laft year of fome fervice in expofing the ignorance and infufficiency of the Minifter, in his aukward attempt at a commercial arrangement with the fifter king-dom; it will be hard if you difpute me that merit, fince my prefent appointment feems fo explicit and fair a confeffion of it on his part. In promoting the coalition between yourfelf and Lord North, you will likewife allow me to have had fome fmall merit, and perhaps, could I have prevailed upon you to lay afide fome old prejudices with regard to my friend Jenkinfon, fecret influence, &c. my talents for negociation might have placed you in the enviable fituation in which Mr.

Pitt

Pitt now ſtands. But I will not inſiſt on this topic, leaſt it ſhould have the appearance of reproaching you with an abſurd and inveterate attachment to certain principles, which, I much fear, it is not in your nature to correct. Unleſs you give me hopes that you are inclined to liſten to the treaty hinted at in the former part of this letter, I doubt, we ſhall be for a conſiderable time ſeparated in our line of public conduct; in that caſe I ſhall be happy to ſee you continue to diſplay thoſe wonderful abilities, of which I have always been a ſincere admirer, in the conduct of Oppoſition. It ever has been my decided opinion (and I now know it by experience) that a conſtitutional oppoſition has its uſe. Should matters turn out leſs agreeably than I flatter myſelf they will, you may depend, my dear Sir, on my returning from Paris preciſely with the ſame principles as thoſe with which I ſet out, and that I ſhall be once more proud to ſubſcribe myſelf

   Your very ſincere,

    and faithful humble ſervant,

       W. E----.

   D

LETTER IV.

To JOHN LEE, *Esq.*

Beckenham, Dec. 7, 1785.

My Dear Lee,

I HAVE this inftant put the finifhing ftroke to a bufinefs, the fortunate refult of which will, I truft, moft agreeably furprife you. But before I proceed to ftate the particulars, let me premife, that I fhould by no means have concluded this important arrangement, without both your opinion on the cafe, and indeed that of my good friend Mrs. Lee, had not I found myfelf indifpenfibly conftrained to do fo, from the aukward circumftance of Mr. Jenkinfon's not having broken the affair to me till near half paft twelve, and yet haftily requiring my decifion at a quarter before one.

To

To rufh at once, as Horace has it, *" in medias res,"* I have acquiefced in Pitt's handfome terms. In a word, my dear Jack, you are henceforth to hail your friend, Commiffarial Envoy and Commercial Regulator to the Court of Verfailles.

Stare as thou wilt, thou honeft Bluntnefs, yet reft affured that I *have* meant, that I *do* mean the whole of this as a liberal fpeculation for the public good. Too great a tendernefs of policy to come at that good, muft in this inftance have inevitably loft my way to it.—But poffibly it may be faid, there is a degree of inconfiftence in this — To which I anfwer, clap your hand on your own heart, Jack, and then refolve me this plaineft of all plain queftions: Are there not cafes where too fcrupulous a predeliction for congruity, may in effect be more intrinfically criminal than the apparently boldeft fuperceffion of them? Yes, yes my friend, the very lapfes of adventurous integrity are venial compared to the pride, the madnefs of falfe firmnefs.

The

The devotion of a feeble frame to the perplexing inveftigation of commercial reci-procity, the complete addiction of a patient underftanding to the intricacy of mercantile detail, the abforption of every faculty, and of every fibre of my mind on this greateft, this deareft concern, may poffibly be fome palliation of an exceffive anxiety upon my part, to give action to idea, and afford effi-cacy to theory. I am frank to own, I *did* moft ardently pant for precifely that poft to which my Sovereign has elected me; but candour requires me to fubjoin, that not wholly unadvifed did his gracious felf, ex-ercife his undoubted prerogative on this try-ing emergency. One of the higheft, and moft dignified characters in this land had pitched on my talents, as exclufively ade-quate to this nice truft. When I acquaint you, that the advifer of our Sovereign upon this grand queftion was no other than my approved friend his Grace of Canterbury, you will applaud both his Majefty's deter-mination and mine.

Yet

Yet with grief I have heard, that tomy acceptance under all the circumstances, your unqualifying apathy exclaimed, " *By my Maker, I'd a seen 'em all damn'd first.*" A strong phrase, my dear Jack; but forgive me, if I say too deeply tinctured with our good old habits of Presbyterian plainness. Let me meet, however, this simplicity of Republican expression, by observing to you, that, on your own grounds, the secret sway of aristocratic tyranny, is to a free-born mind, scarcely less odious than the bolder controul of undisguised despotism.——*I know the Whigs.* Minds, fabricated like ours, Jack, ought not always to surrender up their native enthusiasm to a transmitted creed, or the whim of hereditary talent.

You have here, dear Lee, the faithful portraiture of an honest mind, perhaps indeed too liberal, too independent for the present age, but certainly (with pride I may avow it) unsullied by deceit, unstained by sordid avarice, undegraded by abandoned hypocrisy. Go on, my friend, pursue the generous line you have so righteously adopted. However I may

disapprove

difapprove it on public grounds, I forget its general tendency, in the hope it may conduce to your own private fatisfactions—virtue can always be its own reward; and furely it were hard to grudge fo fimple a remuneration. I have omitted to obferve, that the emoluments of my office are clofe upon fix thoufand pounds *per annum*, exclufive of equipage, plate, fecret fervice money, and other trifling douceurs. Adieu! dear Lee—

Ever your's with truth,

W—— E——.

LETTER

LETTER V.

To *Mr.* WILLIAM WOODFALL.

Beckenham, Dec. 7, 1785.

My Dear Woodfall,

I SIT down to give you *A hasty Sketch of yesterday's business,* leaving it to your own impartiality to make whatever use of it you think fit.

It was somewhat more than half past twelve when Mr. Jenkinson arrived.— —The great conference immediately commenced. To do justice to the profound learning, the admirable judgment, the lively sallies displayed in the course of this interesting argument, would require a much greater memory than any one except yourself, can reasonably be imagined to possess.—Suffice it to acquaint

YOU

you with the agreeable result.—The com-
fortable office of Commercial Ambassador at
Paris is ensured to your friend, with equal
emoluments to the Duke of Dorset's; and,
surely, as must strike your accurate mind,
with superior confidence and credit.—In a
word, the manner of the boon, flowing immediately from the best of Sovereigns, the
adroitness of the Negociator, and the pleas-
ing beneficence of the whole arrangement,
are transporting beyond language to describe.
But now, my dear Billy, I foresee your
shrewd observation—" *How will all this be
reconciled to opposition ?*"

In the first place I must tell you, I have
already written to all their leading men, in
such a way as I think will most probably take
off the edge of their first anger, and in a degree possess them with the idea that I have
merely accepted my office on *public* grounds.
These letters I could wish you to speak of with
your usual kindness.——You will see by the
copies, which I inclose, that I have varied
in my stile, according to the dissimilar characters of my several correspondents. You
will

will therefore extract only such general parts of my defence from these letters, as may be worked up into the most rational paragraphs. Yet I fear there is no dissuading you from touching on my peculiar habits, my information in commerce, my reading, and possibly my scope of mind:—nay, I should not be surprised, if in your friendly way you occasionally drop a few handsome observations on my personal appearance and easy address; which undoubtedly, if in truth you think I possess them, it might not be unadviseable to enlarge on. I would attempt to moderate your friendly enthusiasm, but that I know you will have your own way. One other point I think I could swear you'll urge; I mean your certainty that any man in Opposition would have jumped at what I have taken; and really it is liberal to take that line; as, doubtless, any comparisons of a different nature would only appear invidious, and could answer no good purpose. What I much wish, is to give a pleasant turn to this *apparent* inconsistency—party attachment therefore should be well ridiculed—and I think too, if, in your

E.   pleasant

pleafant ftile, you could, by way of merry illuftration, infinuate that Oppofition had in a manner *lent me* to the Miniftry, for this fpecial purpofe; (juft as your friends, the theatrical managers, accommodate each other by amicable arrangements, on particular emergencies) nothing could be better timed towards the Chriftmas holidays; I defpair of equalling your inimitable ftrokes; but fomething now in this way :

"*His Grace of Dorfet being unavoidably prevented from acting the difficult part of a Commercial Negociator, we underftand Lord North, with his ufual liberality, has permitted Mr. Eden to appear in it for a limited time; and we doubt not, as that promifing performer has undertaken this trying character at a fhort notice, he cannot fail to meet with the loudeft burfts of admiration from a candid and judicious public.*"

Thefe volatile *jeux d'efprit* are always well adapted to parry a ferious reproof, and combat the abfurd violence of national refentment—but I truft all to your plaftic pen.

Be

Be affured, dear Woodfall, I fhall not forget you in my new fituation. It would be too
much to fend you parliamentary fpeeches I
haven't made, when I am known to be at
Paris; but I ftill fhall pen fomething for you,
either in the fhape of panegyric on my new
friends, or as ftrictures on thofe who in future will unreafonably confider me as their
enemy. Befides you fhall receive, for many
years to come, authentic accounts of the
fpeedy determination of my embaffy, with
curious details, documents, and other *folid
ftuff*.

Here is fome tolerable cyder, which, as
our return to England will not be immediate,
I muft intreat you to drink for us, by proxy.
There are alfo a few Goflings of Mrs. E—'s
breeding which wait your acceptance; and
(if through the medium of your friendfhip
I might take the liberty) there is a black
buffalo in our paddock, which brother *Sam-
fon* would infinitely oblige me by giving a
place to in his eligible farm—Every relative
of my friend William's is dear to me.

    Adieu, with cordial attachment
      Ever yours,
          W——— E———.

LETTER VI.

To his Grace the Duke of PORTLAND,
&c. &c.

Beckenham, December 7, 1785.

My Lord,

IT is unneceffary for me to make any apology to your Grace, for troubling you with this letter, to inform you of my acceptance of a commiffion of Minifter Extraordinary and Plenipotentiary, for adjufting a treaty of commerce between this country and France, becaufe I think it my duty to give you the earlieft notice of it, both from gratitude for the favours I have received from your Grace, and on account of the great advantage which will be derived to your party from the engagement which I have now undertaken for the benefit of that Coalition, in the formation of which I took fo large a fhare.

When

When I inform your Grace, that the firſt overture on the ſubjeẟ was accompanied with a ſpontaneous propoſal to ſettle my pay, equipage, &c. upon an equal footing with the Ambaſſador, your diſceinment will ſuggeſt to you the neceſſity of my immediately cloſing with the propoſition, in order to furniſh ſo good a handle to the Oppoſition, for an attack upon the Miniſter, in the enſuing ſeſſion,——At the ſame time I confeſs that I am under much apprehenſion of incurring an imputation of which I have the greateſt horror.—The world may illiberally conceive my conduẟ to proceed from intereſted motives; and though I am ſure to meet with a fair conſtruẟion from your Grace's unſuſpicious and candid mind; yet, as there have been ſo many inſtances of baſe and perfidious apoſtates of late years, I may be claſſed, perhaps, in the number of thoſe mean wretches, and even ſunk to the degrading level of Robinſon, or Lord Delaval. But when I refleẟ on your Grace's noble diſpoſition, and the generous ſpirit of your family, and of the illuſtrious Houſe of Cavendiſh, I truſt that no ſuch miſconſtruẟion

or

cepting the Minifters with whom I am to treat, will confider me as a traitor to my friends and patrons, and a perfon in whom it may not be fafe to repofe any confidence. Your Grace perceives at once how totally fuch fufpicions muft fruftrate the purpofe of my miffion, and render abortive all the idle fchemes of an Adminiftration, who would wifh to patch and trump up a treaty with our perfidious foes. I need not fay that this is for your Grace's private ear. I may now, my Lord, without arrogance, boaft of having returned an effential fervice to that Coalition which placed me in fo elevated and lucrative a ftation, and gave me fuch a leading con-fequence in fome points in the Houfe of Commons.——But whilft I am claiming the merit due to me for rifking, for my friends, every thing that is dear to me (even my good name) let me not be fuppofed to be meanly trying to embrace the benefit which will be derived from having fuch public ground for reprobating the meafure. No, my dear Lord, I am far from expecting any return for thefe fervices; I offered them from grati-

tude,

tude, and only defire that they may not be forgotten, whenever they, or other future events, may produce the effect of overturning an Adminiftration which I have fo repeatedly condemned by motions in the Houfe of Commons.

I have the honour to be,

My LORD,

With the profoundeft fentiments

of refpect and gratitude,

Your Grace's faithful,

and fincere humble fervant,

W——— E———.

LETTER

L E T T E R   VII.

To the Right Honourable

LORD LOUGHBOROUGH, *&c.*

Beckenham, *Dec.* 7, 1785.

My Dear Lord,

ALTHOUGH the unhappy felon who, in your judicial capacity, holds up his hand before you, to anfwer with his life that violation of the law, to which indigence, or perhaps even famine itfelf, may have impelled him, cannot be fuffered to plead his poverty in juftification of his crime, yet, as it is the friend, and not the Chief Juftice I am now addreffing, may I not reafonably hope for fome portion of that mercy, which I am perfuaded, did not your duty as a Judge forbid, your Lordfhip's amiable difpofition would frequently extend to the highwayman, the houfe-breaker, and the pick-pocket.

The

The fimilarity of our fituation is, indeed, ftriking; urged by neceffity, I have, like them, violated the moft facred ties; with this remarkable difference however, that their offences have been perpetrated againft perfons towards whom they have no enmity; whereas mine, with fhame and contrition I acknowledge it, have been committed againft thofe to whom I owed everlafting friendfhip and unbounded gratitude; and with another difference ftill more remarkable, and which I cannot but reflect upon with fenfations of a difagreeable nature, namely, that their evil deeds are generally rewarded with a halter, while mine have been compenfated with an honourable and lucrative employment in the public fervice. To explain the whole of this exordium in a word, I muft acquaint you, my dear Lord, that Mr. Pitt has offered me the appointment of Envoy Extraordinary and Plenipotentiary to Paris, together with the full pay and concomitant emoluments of Ambaffador, which offer, upon the moft mature deliberation, and under all prefent circumftances, I have thought it advifable to accept. I truft you will give

full

full credit to my fincerity, my dear Lord,
when I exprefs the moft poignant concern
in thus fuddenly finding myfelf in a fituation
likely to lead to a difference of opinion on
public matters with you, my earlieft friend
and original patron in public life. But five
children, and a wife who may, in the courfe
of five years, blefs me with as many more,
were arguments in my breaft irrefiftable
againft the rafh and unadvifed rejection of
an income fo truly acceptable as fix thoufand
five hundred pounds a year. In further ex-
tenuation of my conduct, I might perhaps
not unfairly urge the habitual love of bufinefs, and confequent attachment to official
fituation, which your kindnefs, and the pro-
tection and friendfhip of Lord North, had
fo early, and fo powerfully impreffed upon
my mind. Short, very fhort, yet truly te-
dious, has been the period fince my firft
entrance into public life, during which, I
have had the ill fortune to be out of employment; ufe is faid to be a fecond nature, and
my ftrong predilection for office, arifes, no
doubt, from having been fo long accuftom-
ed to the enjoyment of its advantages; if
therefore

therefore I am now guilty of an apparent defertion of my friends, paradoxical as it may feem, to the generous and unmerited excefs of their friendfhip only can it juftly be imputed. Trufting wholly, my dear Lord, to that uniform kindnefs I have experienced from you, to put the moft favourable conftruction on my conduct, I ftill venture to fubfcribe myfelf

Your moft faithful,

devoted, fincere, and grateful

humble fervant and friend,

W——— E———.

LETTER VIII.

To R. B. SHERIDAN, Esq.

My Dear Sheridan,

To men of your enlightened mind and confummate obfervation of human character, profeffion muft always be at once difgufting and fuperfluous.—I fhall not, therefore, indulge myfelf in repeating a detailed inventory of your virtues, nor gratify my friendfhip by telling you what I *could* fay of you—Duplicity is fo common a character in the prefent *æra* of univerfal depravation, that it is the moft difficult attainment in the whole compafs of phyfical practicabilities, to find a man in whofe attachment you can at all depend, or in whofe firmnefs you can repofe any confidence.—Adverfe, however, as I fincerely am to any appearance of profeffions, I cannot refrain from faying this much to you, which

I enter-

I entertain no doubt you will give your moſt implicit belief to, that I feel as ſincere, as warm, as faithful, and as diſinterefted a friendſhip for you as I do for any man breathing.

The immediate reaſon of my writing to you at preſent, is to convince you of my regard, by a teſtimony much more cogent than any aſſertion of mine—the potent evi-dence of actual fact.—In few words, I have finally concluded the negociation which, for the laſt twelve months, has been uni-formly going on, with different degrees of progreſſion between me and Mr. Pitt, and have received the laſt *fiat* to my offi-cial appointment, as Commercial Negoci-ator between this country and France.— Whatever may be the ſentiments of the party on this occaſion (and ſuch is the inſtability of human attachment in theſe times, that I ſhall not wonder if my beſt friends, and thoſe indeed who have ſerved me moſt, were to take the lead againſt me on my preſent pro-motion.) I have at leaſt a peculiar claim upon your gratitude, and an inſuperable pre-
tenſion

tenfion to your approbation.—I need not bring to your recollection the divided intereft we have always taken in one great and important department of Parliamentary bufinefs. We have fought fide by fide, and I think I can, without vanity, affume, that I was not far outdone by you, in the fuccefsful detection of the reiterated inftances of minifterial imbecility, and the diurnal demonftration of th*ir* unexampled ignorance. We conftituted in our two perfons a fpecies of *Hercules Biformes*, vigoroufly and equally engaged in the arduous employment of cleanfing the *Augean* ftable of official corruption and political impurity.

What then will be the confequence of the recent appointment, of which I now convey to you the earlieft information. You will be in your own perfon the fingle man of this conflict, and all the *fame* (of which you know the value better than I pretend to) attached to the victory, will be entirely, and without partition or diminution, your own. For my part, fo you are but benefitted, I am fatisfied; I fubmit to the voluntary degradation

tion of my new commiffion with chearfulnefs,
while I fee my friend and fellow-labourer
gratified and rewarded. If the term *rewarded* fhould feem oddly and uncommonly ufed
in its application to you, let me fuggeft to
you, that the precife meaning of all words
depends upon the circumftances that attend
their introduction, and I am fure, when
compared with the miferable effects that
have accompanied the refult of all my political labours, you will confider your own
fituation as a condition of fplendid and il-
luftrious remuneration indeed. And here
you have the heart of my ftory;—the great
and efficient inftrumentality of my recent
converfion. It was not to ferve the ftate
that I adopted this meafure; for on a careful
revifion of Cay's Abridgment, the happy
fource of my celebrity and difplay, I found
not a fingle word relevant to the fubject of
a commercial treaty between this country
and France. I need not therefore fay to
you, who know me, that no reafonable ex-
pectation of fuperior advantage to my country could influence my determination on this
occafion. It was not to ferve myfelf that I

G   entered

entered into the negociation; for, without vanity, I think I may truly fay, that my regard for myfelf is well known to be as weak and unoperative, as my friendfhip to others is demonftrated to be vigorous, energetic, and · immutable. In fhort, my friend, I did it to ferve you; and I flatter myfelf you will readily agree, few men have gone greater lengths in the indication of their attachment.

If I were in the difpofition to indulge in thofe tepid emanations of genuine humours, thofe dazzling corrufcations of native genius, —thofe flafhes of fplendid colloquy, that are too well known to be the charaĉteriſtic *criteria* of my endowments to make any affeĉtation of modefty on the fubjeĉt at all neceffary, I fhould obferve, that you, as the tutelary patron of *wit*, independent of all operation of gratitude, are bound to become my moft aĉtive advocate in this fituation of poffible acrimony and faĉtious mifreprefentation. For what does the great *Locke* define wit to be? He fays, it is the ready affemblage of two ideas together, which, though *apparently* unlike, are in *reality* not fo.

ſo. Now, does not the union that has taken place between me and Mr. *Pitt* operate, to all intents and purpoſes, as a ſort of practical illuſtration of this definition, and of courſe as a conſequent confirmation of the truth of the theory. For what could for years be more apparently unlike than Mr. Pitt and me ? and yet who, as this event has proved, can ſympathize with a more compleat or accurate veriſimilitude ? One common reſemblance of longitudinal emaciation ; one common poller of literary morbidity ; one common abhorrence of pertinacious and prejudiced adherence to *any* given deſcription of political *catechumen*, one common accuracy in the reminiſcence of original obligation, one common exemption from the weak, though dulcet predominance of official ambition, and one common efferveſcence of perſonal gratitude, may be ſtated as the congenial deſignations of our mutual characters.

Adieu, my dear Sheridan.—Continue to think of me, as I believe you have ever done.—*Vale et plaude.*

Immoveably yours,

W——— E———.

LETTER IX.

To JOSIAH WEDGWOOD, Esq,

Beckenham, Dec. 7, 1785.

DEAR SIR,

I REMEMBER it was an ingenious and judicious obfervation of yours, that the introduction of friendfhip into trade was not lefs abfurd than that of fancy into mathematics: might you not have added, that integrity and politics were equally incompatible? Such at leaft has been my uniform fentiment, and for that reafon I have ever ftudioufly avoided engaging in them, as I am concerned to fay, is the practice of too many, as a profeffion. It is true, that called upon early in life, by the voice of the uninfluenced Electors of the borough of Woodftock to reprefent them in Parliament, I have at different

ferent

ferent times concurred with parties of various
defcriptions; but I have at all times been
particularly attentive, not to bind myfelf
down to any circumfcribed line of political
tenets, which might in any degree deprive
me of that free, unreftrained exercife of my
judgment, which, in my humble apprehen-
fion, a Member of Parliament can never
prudently furrender. In fhort, I flatter myfelf, I fhall not rifque being contradicted
from any quarter, when I venture to affert,
that from my firft entrance into public life,
my conduct has been that of a plain, honeft,
uninfluenced, independent Gentleman; who
without attending to any views, either of
intereft or ambition, has upon all occafions
made the welfare of the community his
fole inviolable rule of action. Such however is the virulence of faction, fuch the
illiberality, and fuch the want of candour
amongft men who concern themfelves in
public affairs, upon motives lefs pure and
difinterefted, that I fhall be little furprized,
to find the ftep I am now about to apprize
you of, malicioufly and induftrioufly reprefented as a defertion of principle, an incon-

fiftency

fiftency of conduct, and an open breach of the moft facred obligations; the ftep I allude to is, that of having accepted from a Minifter, of whom you well know the opinion I entertain, the appointment of Envoy Extraordinary and Plenipotentiary, to conclude a Commercial Treaty between France and Great Britain. Let Malice however do her worft, I flatter myfelf your candour will give me ample credit, when I folemnly proteft and declare, that no confiderations but a fincere and ardent defire to ferve the public interefts in general, and a tender and anxious folicitude for thofe of the manufactures of Great Britain in particular, have had the fmalleft weight in my mind upon the prefent occafion; the trifling and paltry emoluments annexed to the employment, I will confidently affirm cannot be fufpected to have influenced a perfon whofe birth, fortune, and rank in life, have placed him fo infinitely above fuch mean and defpicable temptations: No, my dear Sir, believe me, it is the firm conviction I feel in my own mind, and which I have in a great degree derived from the light of information you

have

have favoured me with, of the utter incapacity of the present Minister, and the scanda-
lous insufficiency and ignorance of all his
Majesty's servants with respect to the commercial interests of the nation, that have decided me to devote my poor abilities to their
service; in the hope of averting some of
those mischiefs which cannot but be expected from their wretched management to befal
this country; I confess I feel at this moment
like a second Curtius (without descending
to a pun upon the subject) devoting myself
to a *Pitt*, for the salvation of my country; I
cannot therefore doubt but you, with all
sincere patriots, will cordially approve my
present conduct.

Before I enter upon the arduous business
I have now undertaken, there is a matter I
wish much to suggest to you, and in which
should I be so fortunate as to have your con-
currence, I shall esteem myself peculiarly
happy. Conversant as you are in the manu-
facturing interest, it is needless to point out
to you, that whatever treaty I may conclude
with the Cabinet of Versailles, it cannot be
expected

expected to prove equally beneficial to all
the different branches of them, and confe-
quently I am not to flatter myfelf with an
univerfal approbation of the refult by my
negociations; (I truft I need hardly fay, that
Earthen ware will not be the article to which
I fhall be the leaft attentive.) This circumftance being duly confidered, I confefs it
ftrikes me, and hope it will appear in the
fame light to you, that no future meetings
of the Chamber of Commerce can poffibly
be attended with any advantage to the public; I will therefore take leave to recom-
mend it moft earneftly to you, to ufe your
moft ftrenuous endeavours to prevent any
future affemblies of that kind; it was but
too evident from the little fuccefs we had,
on this fide of the water, in our oppofition
to the Irifh Propofitions, that our utmoft
efforts againft the will of the Minifter muft
in the prefent Parliament prove ineffectual ;
and I own I am not without hope, that the
general good opinion I have been anxious to
eftablifh of my fincere concern for the ma-
nufacturing intereft, will difpofe all parties

to

to rely implicitly on my moſt ſtrenuous exertions for the common proſperity of all.—
One thing I would authoriſe you to promiſe,
in my name, to every diſtinᴄt branch of our
manufaᴄtures, namely, that I will not, on
any account whatever, haſtily or precipitately
conclude any treaty which may affeᴄt their
intereſt; I care not how much of my time
I ſacrifice to their ſervice, and though the
buſineſs I am now undertaking ſhould de-
tain me from my native country, and the
enjoyment of my domeſtic comfort, five, or
even ten years, rather than negleᴄt their
intereſts in the minuteſt particular, I will
patiently and chearfully ſubmit to my lot.—
For them and their ſakes only, I become a
voluntary exile; for them I expoſe my cha-
raᴄter to the moſt odious and ignominious
imputations. Do I aſk too much, when, in
return, I requeſt only their confidence in my
deſire to ſerve them, and a ſuppreſſion of
thoſe meetings, which however wiſe, while
their concerns were in the hands of ignorance and incapacity, become unneceſſary,
if not prejudicial, when they are entruſted to

H   one

one in whole zeal and exertion they may realonably confide?

I am, dear Sir,

With the greateſt eſteem and regard,

Your very faithful,

and devoted humble ſervant,

W. E——.

P. S. As my reſidence on the Continent may probably be long, I will trouble you to give orders to your principal agent, to countermand the three dozen chamber utenſils I had beſpoke, with the figure of Mr. Pitt engraved in the bottom of them; for which I am happy to learn, you have had ſo extenſive a demand, as I was ſo lucky as to be the perſon who originally ſuggeſted the idea of them.

LETTER X.

To WILLIAM ADAM, Esq. M. P.

Beckenham, Kent, n. 2, 1786.

DEAR ADAM,

THERE have been hitherto so many circumstances of common sympathy between you and me, in the course of our pursuits in life, that I think it particularly my duty to comment on the first instance of its interruption, and to reprehend you gently for the voluntary deviation from the standard of our original friendship, of which I am not unapprized, by the objection which I understand you have expressed to my conduct in a recent instance of my good fortune. You set out in your career of politics under the cheering auspices of Lord North ;—so did I. You were an active and warm friend

II 2   to

to the Coalition ;—·ſo was I. You have an amiable and deſerving wife, together with a large family ;—ſo have I. You were originally bred to the profeſſion of the law ;— ſo was I. Why then will you not permit me to add to this detail of affirmative reſemblances, an equally congenial liſt of contraries ; and allow me to ſay, you have left Lord North, as well as I. You have abandoned the Coalition, juſt as I have done.— You have deſerted the drudgery of an ignoble profeſſion for the attainment of more rapid emolument, and in that alſo have followed the example of your friend.———— Why will you give me an opportunity, even for the moſt lenient rebuke on the ſubject of violated conſiſtency and injured ſympathy.— Think better of it.

Will you permit me to ſpeak to my new allies, to obtain for you the employment of Commercial Negociator between this country and the Court of Madrid ? The office is as neceſſary, in point of fact, as mine ; and has this advantage, that it cannot be expoſed to the empty ridicule of factious jibers, on

the

the fcore of there being two Plenipotentiaries
at the fame Court. The moft ingenious of
them cannot prove that.——Might it not,
however, facilitate your appointment, and
reconcile an inquifitive, difcontented multi-
tude to the extravagance, as they may call
it, of your nomination, if you were to move
profeffionally for a writ of enquiry, to dif-
cover a true ftate of the Ambaffador's
locality, and to afcertain the moot point of
his exiftence. This writ, you know, lies
legally in all cafes of *nihil decit*, or *non eft
informatus*; and on each of thefe accounts,
both as to taciturnity, and the abfence of
information, what judicature will queftion
the fingular propriety of its iffuing againft
fuch an individual as the Earl of Chefter-
field? As another mode of effecting the
fame purpofe, for the little Earl has been
evidently reprefented in the *Retorna* BRE-
VIUM (pardon this fimple inftance of the
paronamafia) as a *ncn eft inventxs*, may it
not be practicable to iffue a *latitat*?——a pro-
cefs which indeed owes its name to the fup-
pofition that the defendant doth " lurk and
lie hid," to compel him to anfwer to his
duty,

delicacy!—Nay, so much am I satisfied of
the full and unqualified sincerity of his opinion upon the case, that I am convinced,
were I to go down to the House on the first
day of its meeting, to take a place, impof-
fible as such an hypothesis must appear, on
the adverse side of the House, or even to
seat myself between a couple of the most
abandoned and convicted profligates in the
records of political delinquency, he would
even, under such circumstances, honour me
with his notice, and indulge himself in the
most unambiguous eulogia upon the expe-
diency and necessity of my official promo-
tion, and upon the purity and disinterested-
ness of my personal inducements—need I
say mine—His opinion will, I trust, influence yours, and I doubt not of their entire
coincidence.

I will only add, that though bred a lawyer,
I am not implacable—that though no longer
a whig in personal connection, I am so sin-
cerely attached to that principle in the theory
of their creed, *inimicitiæ placabiles*, that I
here give you full authority to assure your
friends,

friends, that if either the French Court
fhould demur to my appointment, or by any
other odd flaw, I fhould fuffer a non-fuit at
home, I fhall in that cafe be quite willing
to forego all actions of battery or trefpafs,
which it is my prefent duty to inftitute and
carry on againft them, and to join iffue with
them with as much good faith and genuine
attachment as ever.

Believe me, Dear Adam,

to be conftantly and inviolably yours,

W——— E——.

P. S.   Pray do you happen to know any
thing in the way of your profeffion (for I
underftand he is an attorney, and may therefore occafionally vifit you with a brief) of
Mr. Sayer, the famous fatirift of our modern
politics? if you do, I wifh you would inti-
mate to him the propriety of omitting me
in the future editions of his juftly celebrated

print, called, The Concerto Co-alitionali.—
You may tell him, I no longer belong to
that Band. I had no idea of playing when
I saw so little chance of the piper being paid
—*volto subito* therefore was the word—and I
changed my key—I have indeed raised my
pitch through the whole compass of the
diapason, from the deep grumbling note of
Faction to the *alto* of ambassadorship.—Let
him know this, he will perceive I understand
time, and will acknowledge also, I trust,
that I did well to relinquish a company of
gentlemen performers, who volunteer their
exertions to gain a set so thoroughly devoted to the art they possess, that like Nero,
they can fiddle even when their country is
undoing.

F I N I S.

www.ingramcontent.com/pod-product-compliance
Lightning Source LLC
Chambersburg PA
CBHW030859260626
47169CB00008B/2595